SPIDER'S CHRISTMAS GIFT

Melissa Kajpust

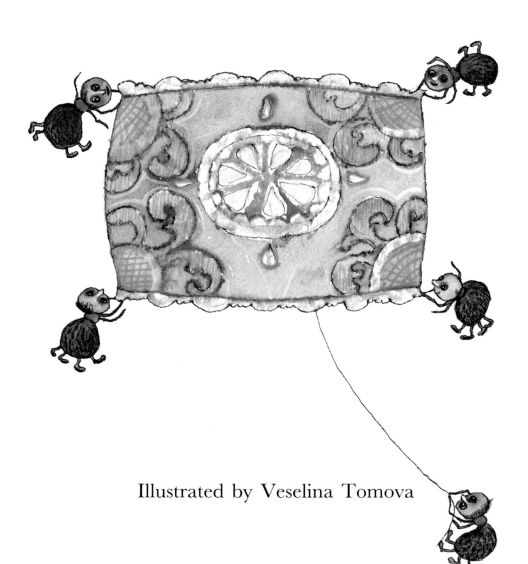

Illustrated by Veselina Tomova

VIKING

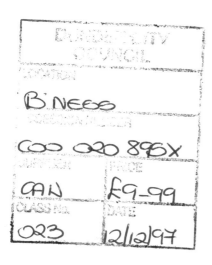

VIKING

Published by the Penguin Group
Penguin Books Ltd, 27 Wrights Lane, London W8 5TZ, England
Penguin Books USA Inc., 375 Hudson Street, New York, New York 10014, USA
Penguin Books Australia Ltd, Ringwood, Victoria, Australia
Penguin Books Canada Ltd, 10 Alcorn Avenue, Toronto, Ontario, Canada M4V 3B2
Penguin Books (NZ) Ltd, 182–190 Wairau Road, Auckland 10, New Zealand

Penguin Books Ltd, Registered Offices: Harmondsworth, Middlesex, England

First published in the USA by Hyperion Books for Children 1993
This edition published by Viking by arrangement with Hyperion Books for Children 1995

Text copyright © Melissa Kajpust, 1993
Illustrations copyright © Veselina Tomova, 1993

The moral right of the author and illustrator has been asserted

Manufactured in China by Imago Publishing Ltd

A CIP catalogue record for this book is available from the British Library
ISBN 0–670–85995–8

For Daniel, Holly and David

A long time ago, a mother spider
lived with her forty tiny children
in a stable outside Bethlehem.

The mother spider was gentle and loving.
Her many children kept her busy, yet she was
always willing to help others if they needed
her. When the lamb broke its leg, the mother
spider spun a web round and round to form
a strong and sturdy cast.

When the roof leaked directly over the donkey's stall, the mother spider plugged the hole with mud and grass that she joined with silk threads. All the animals appreciated her special care.

One evening a brilliant star lit up the sky and shone directly over the stable. "What does it mean?" the little spiders asked their mother.

"I don't know," she replied, "but surely it must signify something wonderful."

That same evening a young woman named Mary came to the stable. She and her husband, Joseph, sought shelter because they could find no other place.

Soon Mary gave birth to a baby boy and called him Jesus. The spiders and the other animals watched quietly as the young mother wrapped the child in soft blankets and laid him in a manger filled with straw.

The little spiders wanted to visit the new baby as they had visited all the other new babies that were born in the stable. The mother spider forbade them. "You may frighten the baby and his mother," she said. "Most people don't like spiders, and some harm may come to you." Grudgingly her children crawled back to their nest under the cattle trough.

"I don't scare people," protested one young spider.

Cautiously he crawled out of the nest, past his sleeping brothers and sisters, determined to see the new child.

He moved quickly up the wall and along the rafter and stopped directly over the manger, where the baby lay sleeping, tended by Mary.

The little spider could not see clearly from
his position, so he moved closer to the edge.
He stretched his eight skinny legs out as far
as he could, until his tiny knobbly knees began
to quiver and his small round furry body
began to shake.

When he stretched again he could no longer hold on. Down he fell, right into the manger, beside the sleeping baby. When he opened his eyes and shook the dizziness out of his head, he saw that Mary was peering down at him.

He heard her easy laughter. She reached into the manger, carefully scooped him up in her hand, and told him to scurry home. The mother spider was annoyed with her child and scolded him for not obeying her.

The little spider was on his way back to bed when he saw three men in flowing robes enter the stable. They had come to visit Mary and had brought rich gifts for the baby.

The little spider asked, "Can we give the baby a present, too?"

"I'm grateful for the woman's kindness, but what shall we give?" his mother replied sadly. "We have nothing."

Suddenly she had an idea! She awakened all her children and gathered them around her to tell them her plan.

Far into the night, while her children spun
silk, the mother spider wove all the threads
together. They finished just as the sun's rays
stretched over the horizon.

25

A dozen silk coverlets glimmered in the early morning light. The mother spider folded them carefully and asked the lamb to help move them to where the baby and his mother slept.

When Mary awoke she was delighted with the gift. She thought they were the most beautiful coverlets she had ever seen. But where did they come from? By chance she looked up to the rafter, where she saw the mother spider and all her children watching her. Then she remembered the little spider. "Thank you," she said. "You have made a lovely gift for my baby. Please come closer and see him."

The spiders gathered along the edge of the manger to gaze at the sleeping child. The adventurous young spider, however, climbed up the wall beside the manger and sat on the edge of the small window for his glimpse of the baby.

A long shaft of light touched the corner of
the stall where the rich gifts were placed.
The little spider saw the gold and jewels and
sweet-scented spices. But now in the very
centre were the shimmering silk coverlets.